Antonia had loved horses for as long as she could remember.

For Bonney,
who loved the carousel when she was a girl

RETURNING NICHOLAS

Deborah Durland DeSaix

FARRAR STRAUS GIROUX   NEW YORK

Published simultaneously in Canada by HarperCollins Canada Ltd
Printed and bound in the United States of America
by Worzalla
Designed by Amy Samson
First edition, 1995

Library of Congress Cataloging-in-Publication Data
DeSaix, Deborah Durland.
p.   cm.
Returning Nicholas / Deborah Durland DeSaix. — 1st ed.
[1. Merry-go-round—Fiction.   2. Horses—Fiction.]   I. Title.
PZ7.D44887Re   1995   [E]—dc20   94-30328   CIP   AC

She'd never ridden before, but she imagined galloping
across the prairie on her trusty Appaloosa, or jumping huge
fences in a steeplechase.

One afternoon, she noticed that a small carnival had been set up in a field near her house, and right in the middle of the tents and trucks was a carousel full of horses.

An old woman was polishing the painted horses with a cloth. "You can have the first ride of the day," she said.

Antonia's eyes lit up. The russet horse seemed more spirited than the rest, so she climbed on it and picked up the reins. The carousel music began . . .

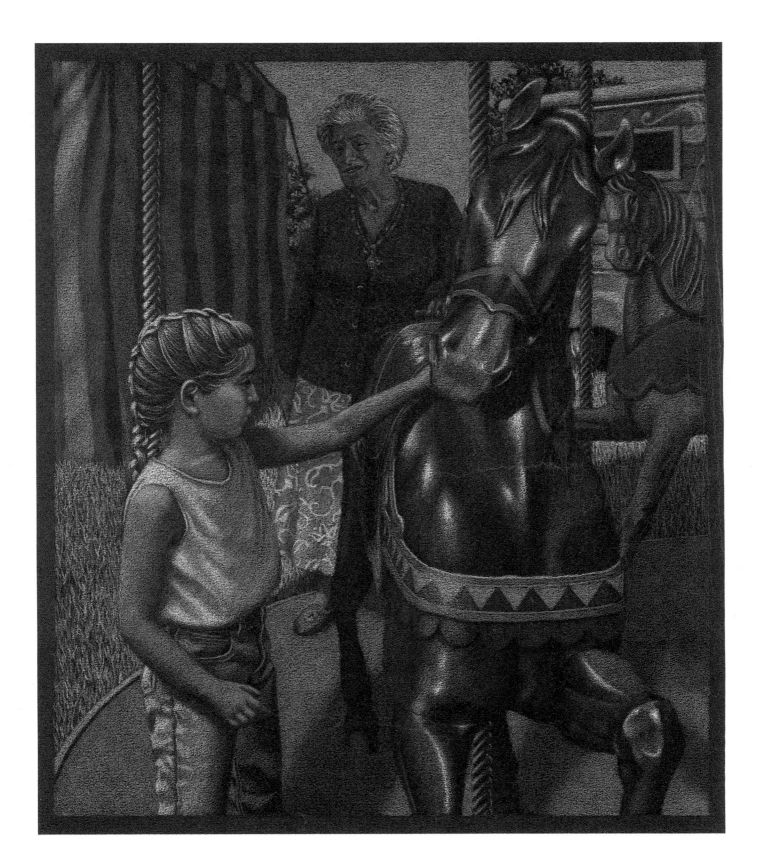

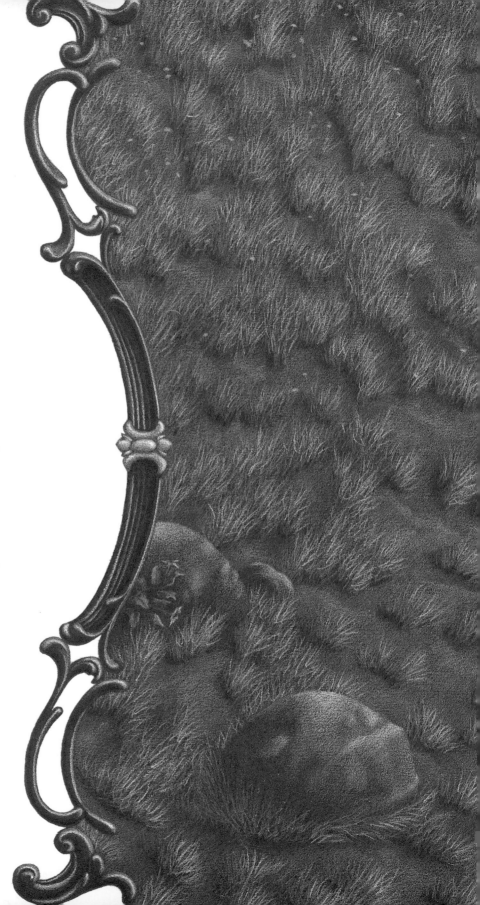

. . . and to her surprise she
found herself on the broad
back of a real horse. Antonia
laughed, then leaned forward in
the saddle and gripped tightly
with her knees, just the way she
had seen in books.

"Where are we going?"
Antonia asked the horse. She
tried pulling on the reins, and the
horse slowed down. When she
saw a narrow dirt road, she
tugged gently on the reins and
the horse turned toward it. As
they cantered downhill,
Antonia thought she heard
faint music.

All of a sudden she was back on the wooden horse. The carousel had stopped.

She saw the woman in the middle of the carousel. "This horse," Antonia said, "it's really special."

The woman walked over. She looked closely at Antonia and then nodded. "I think so, too," she said. "My grandfather carved these horses many years ago. You were riding Nicholas."

The next day, Antonia ran through pouring rain to the carnival. The old woman stood just inside a tent.

"You're our only visitor today," she said to Antonia. "I can give you a very long ride."

Antonia went straight to Nicholas. She took a deep breath
as the carousel started to turn. The first notes of music
sounded . . .

. . . and her horse raced up the dirt road. She reined him to a stop at the crest of the hill. Far ahead were three brightly painted horse-drawn wagons. Antonia looked down at her horse's colorful trappings.

"I bet you belong to them," she said, stroking his mane. He
turned his head and gazed back at her. As the wagons
disappeared slowly into a forest, she urged the horse forward.

Night was falling when she
and the horse reached the
trees. It became very dark.
"Don't worry," Antonia said.
"That must be them up ahead."
She slid to the ground and led
him toward a distant campfire.

They walked between two wagons into the circle of light. A young girl ran up to them. "Nicholas, you bad horse!" she scolded.

"My name is Magda," she said to Antonia. "You're very kind to bring our horse back. He was frightened by a snake and threw my grandfather off. We looked and looked, but Nicholas was gone. Come and tell me how you found him."

As Antonia told her tale, Magda's eyes grew large.

"My grandfather is making carvings of all our horses," Magda said. "He's going to build them a carousel, and we'll travel from town to town with it. He's working on the carving of Nicholas now."

"I'm putting my heart into those carvings," said the old man as he joined them. "Thank you for returning Nicholas. I couldn't have finished without him."

He took the reins from Antonia. "You must love horses
very much," he said. "Nicholas allows only me to ride him."
Antonia stood, reached out, and stroked Nicholas's nose.

Then, very far away, she heard notes of carousel music.
Suddenly Nicholas, Magda, and her grandfather were gone
and she was standing beside the painted carousel horse.

The next morning, Antonia hurried through her chores and raced to the carousel. When she reached the field, it was empty. The carnival trucks were pulling away down the street, but one still sat at the curb. The woman who ran the carousel got out and walked over to Antonia.

She put in Antonia's hand a carving of a girl on a horse. "My grandfather made that for you," the old woman said, smiling gently. "I never thought I would have to wait so long to give it to you."